D1469095

David Bedford was born in Devon, in the southwest of England, in 1969.

David wasn't always a writer – first he was a soccer player! He played for two teams: Appleton Football Club and Sankey Rangers. Although these weren't the worst teams in the league, they never won anything! David was also a scientist. His first job was in the United States, where he worked on discovering new antibiotics.

But, David always loved to read and he decided to start writing stories himself. After a few years, he left his job as a scientist and began writing full time. He now has 10 books published, which have been translated into many languages around the world.

David lives with his wife and daughter in Norfolk, England.

Keith Brumpton has written and illustrated over 35 humorous books for children. He also writes scripts and screenplays. Keith now lives in Glasgow, Scotland.

To my Uncle Fred Jones, for taking me
to the games — thanks mate.
DB

First American Edition 2006
by Kane/Miller Book Publishers, Inc.
La Jolla, California

First published in 2003 by Little Hare Books, Australia
Text copyright © David Bedford 2003
Illustrations copyright © Keith Brumpton 2003

Kane/Miller Book Publishers, Inc.
P.O. Box 8515
La Jolla, CA 92038-8515
www.kanemiller.com

Library of Congress Control Number: 2005930841
Printed and bound in China by Regent Publishing Services Ltd.
1 2 3 4 5 6 7 8 9 10

ISBN-13: 978-1-933605-01-2
ISBN-10: 1-933605-01-4

DAVID BEDFORD

Illustrated by Keith Brumpton

Kane/Miller
BOOK PUBLISHERS

Chapter 1

Harvey raced back to The Team's goal to defend, scrunching his shoulders against the rain, which was like a waterfall drumming on his head.

He saw Darren, The Team goalie, wipe his eyes, leaving long streaks of mud across his face. The rain had turned the goal area into a swamp, and Darren's feet had sunk up to his ankles as he crouched, ready to dive.

The Rovers forward outran Matt and Steffi and the rest of The Team defense. Harvey put on one last burst of speed, but he was too late. The forward flicked a shot over Darren's head.

Darren jumped. At least, he tried to. But the sticky mud held his feet as if they were stuck in concrete. He fell over backwards, and The Team watched the ball sail towards the goal.

Harvey groaned. It was 0–0, with only five minutes to go, and Darren had just missed a shot he should have easily saved.

Luckily, the ball hit the crossbar — DONK!

— and rebounded away for a corner kick. "Phew!" Darren sighed in relief as he pulled his feet out of the mud. Matt and Steffi were furious, though.

"You mudbrain!" shouted Steffi. "They nearly scored!"

"You didn't even dive!" screamed Matt. "This is the biggest game we've ever played, remember?"

The Team had been getting better all season, climbing slowly towards the top of the league. They needed just one more point to be sure of winning the league trophy — and a trip to Soccer Camp.

"You try goalkeeping in a swamp!" Darren yelled back at Matt and Steffi.

"You try keeping your eyes open, swampman!" said Steffi.

Before Darren could reply, the ball was kicked high from the corner. Darren launched himself into the air to catch it. Steffi, Matt and two Rovers forwards jumped to head it. They all missed the ball, and Rita kicked it up the field for Harvey to chase.

"Wait!" shouted Rita, and everyone stopped. "Where's Darren?"

Harvey put his foot on the ball and looked around. There was no one in goal.

"He was there when the ball came over," said Rita. "Then he just ... disappeared!"

SLUUUUURCH!

A shape rose up from the swamp. Brown water and lumps of mud ran down its arms and fell from the fingers of its goalkeeper's gloves. The thing slowly opened its eyes.

"Darren!" said Rita. "Are you all right?"

Darren nodded, and a lump of mud the size of an orange rolled off his head and landed at his feet with a plop.

"I told you to keep your eyes open!" scolded Steffi.

"Great dive!" snorted Matt. "But you should take your cleats off *before* you go swimming!"

As the rain washed the mud from Darren's face, Harvey saw that there were angry purple splotches on his cheeks.

"Two minutes to go!" the referee called.

Harvey suddenly remembered the ball at his feet. The Rovers midfielders, who had stopped to stare at Darren, were closing in on him. He spun away from them and sprinted towards the Rovers' goal. He swerved past one defender, then another. But the third one tackled him, and the Rovers were back on the attack.

Harvey was running back to defend when he saw it happen.

Darren was still arguing with Steffi and Matt.

No one was paying any attention to the game.

"Look out!" cried Harvey.

It was too late. The Rovers forward shot, and Darren didn't even see the ball as it flew past his knee and into the net for a goal.

The ref blew the final whistle. For the first
time in months, The Team had lost.

"Oh, you're USELESS!" Steffi shouted at
Darren.

"WORSE than useless!" yelled Matt.

Darren pushed past them without speaking
and stormed off across the field.

"Darren!" called Harvey. "Don't go! It wasn't your fault!"

"Of course it was his fault," said Matt. "He's supposed to be our ace goalie. He couldn't even catch a cold."

Darren turned to yell, "I don't care! I've had ENOUGH!"

It looked like the purple splotches on Darren's cheeks had spread over his whole face.

"We're better off without him," said Steffi.
"Anyway, we've still got one more game and
one more chance to win. We'll just find
someone else to go in goal. No one could be
worse than Darren."

"We don't need anyone else in goal," said
Harvey angrily. "Darren is The Team goalie.
He's saved us plenty of times, so give him a
break!"

"I'll talk to Darren," said Rita. "I'm sure
he'll come back."

But Harvey wasn't so sure. He'd never seen
anyone get so upset that they grew purple
splotches on their face. Harvey didn't think
Darren would come back — ever.

Chapter 2

Harvey trudged home through the puddles. Waves of water gushed from his soggy cleats, but he hardly noticed.

He was worried about The Team. They used to be the worst in the league. Then Harvey's neighbor, Professor Gertie, had invented Mark 1, the Soccer Machine.

With Mark 1's coaching help, The Team were now on their way to being the best in the league.

At first, winning had been the most fun Harvey and The Team had ever had.

Then, things started to change. The closer they got to the top of the league, the more they argued.

Harvey was worried about something else, too. Mark 1 and Professor Gertie should have been at the game to cheer The Team on. What could have happened to them?

Harvey turned onto Baker Street, squished up the hill to the top, and stopped at Professor Gertie's inventing tower.

The tower rose tall and straight into the gray sky, like a rocket about to take off. Harvey knocked on the door.

He heard shouting, then feet stomping on metal stairs. Finally, the door was yanked open and Professor Gertie stood there, red-faced and glowering.

"Oh, hello Harvey," she said, trying not to sound as angry as she looked. "How are you today?"

"You missed the game," said Harvey. "And we lost."

Normally, Professor Gertie would have wanted to know all about the game, but now she simply shook her head. "I lost track of time," she muttered. "I'm sorry, Harvey. Come on up."

Harvey followed her up the twisting stairs into the tower. "Who was shouting?" he asked.

Professor Gertie frowned. "That was me," she admitted. "Mark 1 has stopped doing what he's told. He keeps arguing."

"Just like The Team," said Harvey, and he explained about Darren storming off.

"If I could invent a cure for arguing, I'd be rich," said Professor Gertie gloomily. "The problem is, there's no quick fix."

Harvey was disappointed. Inventors were always coming up with quick fixes. He thought that's what inventors were for.

Harvey found Mark 1 in the living room. He was the perfect soccer machine. He had a top speed of 35 miles per hour, a Spinner for turning, Skidders for braking, and Bouncing Boots for jumping. The brain inside his trashcan head was dedicated purely to soccer.

At the moment, Mark 1 was lying on the couch, watching cartoons.

"Hey," said Harvey.

"Ho," said Mark 1, giving Harvey a friendly flash of his red laser eyes before turning back to the television.

"I don't know what's wrong with him," whispered Professor Gertie. "When he's not out coaching The Team, he sulks in his room or watches television. He won't listen to anything I say."

"Maybe his ears aren't working!"

"I checked," said Professor Gertie. "His Listeners are fine. He's *pretending* not to hear. Watch."

She picked up her Shouting Mask from the top of the television and strapped it over her mouth. The Shouting Mask was another of Professor Gertie's inventions. It amplified her voice so she sounded like a thousand people shouting at once. Now she'd found a new use for it. She bellowed,

"Mark 1! Take your feet off the couch!

Mark 1! Clean up your room!

Mark 1! Why don't you answer me WHEN I'M TALKING TO YOU?!!!"

Harvey had to cover his ears. He could easily guess why Mark 1 was pretending not to hear.

"Don't you think," he asked Professor Gertie carefully, "that you might be, just a little bit, nagging him?"

Professor Gertie, who was still wearing the Shouting Mask, looked like a giant, angry duck. **"Me? Nagging? Of course not! All I'm asking is for Mark 1 to be a bit tidier and**

DO AS I SAY! It's all right for *him* — going out and coaching The Team and enjoying himself. I'm the one who has to stay at home washing his socks and tidying up and doing so many other things that I don't even have time for my inventions!"

Mark 1 flashed his eyes at Harvey again, then tied one of his socks over his earholes and started bouncing his boots up and down on the couch.

Professor Gertie carried on nagging Mark 1 through her Shouting Mask.

Harvey, with his hands still covering his ears, left them to it. If Professor Gertie couldn't help, he would have to fix The Team's problems himself.

As he left the tower he saw Rita running up the hill.

"I talked to Darren," she called out. "He's not angry now!"

"That's great!" said Harvey. But Rita didn't look happy.

"Actually, it's not great," she said. "Because he still doesn't want to come back. He said playing on The Team gave him purple splotches, and it wasn't fun anymore."

Harvey sighed. "We're the problem," he said," not Darren." We've got to stop The Team from arguing. But Professor Gertie said there are no quick fixes."

"So what are we going to do next Saturday?" asked Rita. "It's our last game, and it's against the Diamonds."

"The best team in the league," said Harvey gloomily.

"Except for The Team," said Rita. "And we still only need one point to win the trophy."

Harvey sighed. "Without a goalie we won't have a chance."

Rita reached into her back pocket and brought out two soggy goalkeeper's gloves.

"Darren gave me these. I'm willing to go in goal if I have to."

Harvey brightened. "Are you any good?"

"No," said Rita. "I stink."

Chapter 3

"You're not that bad," said Harvey.

Rita and Harvey had practiced every night since Saturday. Now it was Thursday, and the rest of The Team would be showing up soon for their practice with Mark 1. For the first time in a week, it had stopped raining.

"Try this." Harvey kicked the ball towards the goal. Rita jumped to catch it, but the ball slipped through her hands.

"Told you," she said. "I stink."

Harvey tried an even slower shot, rolling the ball along the ground. Rita bent down and gathered it up, but the ball knocked hard against her chin and Harvey heard her teeth rattle.

"You okay?" asked Harvey.

"I jutht bit my tongue," said Rita, with a grimace. "Take another thot."

"My turn!" Steffi raced onto the field, intercepted the ball and kicked it easily into the goal.

"You've got to watch what's going on," Steffi said. "That was Darren's problem, too."

"Don't tell me what to do," said Rita, marching out of the goal towards Steffi.

Suddenly there was a shout. "Yoo-hooo!" They all turned to see Professor Gertie hurrying across the field with Mark 1, who was carrying a box.

As they drew near, the box slipped from Mark 1's hands.

"Did you see that?" Rita whispered. "Mark 1 dropped it on purpose."

"They're not getting along," replied Harvey.

Professor Gertie looked at Mark 1 crossly, then picked up two of her inventions. "You didn't think I'd let you down, did you?" she asked, turning to Rita. "I put the housework on hold and directed all my efforts towards these. Mark 1 helped, by doing what he was TOLD for a change!"

Harvey and Rita examined the inventions. They looked to Harvey like the kind of gloves King Arthur and his knights wore, except that each finger had a suction cup on the end.

"They're Anti-Goal Gauntlets!" said Professor Gertie, beaming.

As the rest of The Team arrived, Rita pulled off her old goalkeeper's gloves and Professor Gertie pushed the gauntlets on.

"They're heavy," Rita said.

"I had to use armor-plated steel," Professor Gertie explained. "So the Finger Rockets don't burn through."

"Finger Rockets?" asked Rita nervously.

"They shoot out when you stretch your fingers wide. Try it!"

Rita stood in goal, holding the heavy gloves as far away from her body as she could. She didn't like the sound of Finger Rockets.

"Ready, set, go!" called Professor Gertie excitedly.

"Let me shoot," said Steffi with a mischievous grin. She took a long run up, and fired the ball, shouting "Goal!" as soon as the ball had left her foot.

Rita reached for the ball, stretching her
fingers wide.

The Anti-Goal Gauntlets started to vibrate
and grow hot. Then there were eight tiny puffs
of smoke, and eight tiny screams as the gloves'
fingertips shot out like fireworks.

Three of them hit the ball and stuck.

The fingertips were still attached to Rita's gloves by elastic bands. She yanked her wrists, and the ball sprang easily towards her. She caught it between both hands and called, "Saved!"

Everyone except Steffi cheered.

Professor Gertie peeled the suction cups from the ball. "Now clap your hands," she said. "The elastic bands will wind back in so the Finger Rockets are ready to fire again."

Rita clapped. Nothing happened.

She clapped harder. Still, nothing happened.

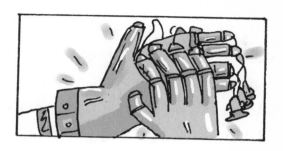

Professor Gertie stared dangerously at Mark 1. "Did you put the Winders in like I told you to?"

Mark 1 pretended not to hear.

Professor Gertie's eyes nearly popped out of her head. She drew in a huge breath, but before she could shout, Harvey asked hastily, "What about your other inventions?"

Professor Gertie let her breath out in a long sigh. "Well, okay," she said, giving Mark 1 a final glare. "But the Finger Rockets were my favorite."

She picked up another pair of gloves from the ground.

Rita took off the Anti-Goal Gauntlets and put the new gloves on. They didn't seem unusual at all, except for a coil of wire like an aerial stitched around each finger, and a tiny satellite dish on the end of each thumb.

"Sit down," said Professor Gertie. Harvey watched curiously as she screwed something to the bottom of Rita's cleats. Now the cleats looked like rollerskates, but instead of wheels, each one had a red-and-white striped skirt.

"Are they ... *hovercrafts*?" asked Harvey.

"I call them Gliders," said Professor Gertie as she pulled Rita to her feet. "When Rita reaches for the ball, her thumbs will tell the Gliders which way to go. And the gloves have Sticky Palms — but don't worry about that now."

Harvey lined up the ball, and Rita clomped clumsily to the center of the goal. The Gliders were so heavy she could barely lift her feet.

"Ready?" asked Harvey. Rita nodded, and he kicked the ball high towards the goal.

Rita reached out her hands. Suddenly, she started to glide. As she sailed quickly across the goal mouth, the ball hit her gloves — and stuck.

"The Sticky Palms work!" said Professor Gertie.

"Let's try it again!" said Rita. She went to throw Harvey the ball — but it stayed firmly stuck to her gloves.

Professor Gertie turned to Mark 1. "Did you mix some Anti-Sticky in with the Sticky so that the ball would come unstuck? I remember telling you to!"

Mark 1 pretended not to hear, but Harvey saw a gleam of triumph flash across his laser eyes.

"Rats!" shouted Professor Gertie. "You've ruined all my inventions — and they worked, too!" Harvey thought she was going to explode like a Finger Rocket.

"They were awesome," he said quickly. "But we can't use them on Saturday. The ref doesn't allow inventions."

Professor Gertie pulled the sticky gloves off Rita and, with Rita's and Harvey's help, tugged the ball free.

Harvey stood out of the way as she threw all her useless inventions back into their box. He had never seen her so grumpy before.

"Let's give Rita some more practice," Harvey said encouragingly.

"Good idea," said Matt. "She needs it!"

"She *really* needs it!" scoffed Steffi.

Rita put on Darren's regular goalkeeper's gloves, and Mark 1 started firing shots at the goal. She didn't even save one.

"We're going to get hammered," groaned Steffi. "Rita's completely useless!"

Rita took off her gloves. "Find yourself another goalie, then," she said, and walked off across the field.

Matt turned to Steffi. "That's the second goalie you've scared away! Why don't you give everyone a break?"

"You started it!" said Steffi.

"You did, you mean!" said Matt.

Soon everyone was shouting.

Harvey watched Rita cross the field. She passed Professor Gertie and Mark 1, who were picking up the box Mark 1 had just dropped again. Professor Gertie was shouting as well.

"That's it!" Harvey bellowed. "The Team are FINISHED!"

But everyone was arguing so loudly that no one heard him.

Chapter 4

That night, Harvey had a dream. In it, he was Professor Harvey, and he lived in an inventing tower full of his own shiny, brilliant inventions.

It wasn't a pleasant dream, though. All day, people kept knocking on his door, begging him to fix their problems and arguing with him when he said he didn't know how.

"We used to like playing together," they said. "But now we hate it!"

"There's too much pressure! It's making us too nervous!"

They all had purple splotches on their faces.

Professor Harvey scratched his head, thinking. Suddenly, he had an idea. It was perfect! And so simple! Why hadn't he thought of it before?

Harvey woke up. His alarm clock was ringing, and his bedroom was filled with bright sunlight. In his dream, Professor Harvey had just thought of a way to stop people from arguing. If only Harvey could remember what it was.

He lay back on his bed and closed his eyes, trying to get back into the dream. But he couldn't.

He sat up again. Whenever Professor Gertie was trying to solve a problem, she wrote a list. Harvey grabbed one of his school notebooks and opened it to a fresh page.

He tried to imagine he really *was* Professor Harvey. He scratched his head like Professor Harvey had, and pretended his bedroom was Professor Harvey's inventing room. But he couldn't think of anything to write. Instead, he doodled a face in the corner of the page. He gave the face a shock of hair like Darren's. Then he drew splotches all over the face.

The Team were nervous because they wanted to win so badly. Their nerves were making them argue — and their arguing was making their nerves even worse.

Harvey put his pen to the top of the page and wrote, "How to Stop Arguing and Be a Team."

Then he wrote a list. Maybe if he showed it to Professor Gertie she could use it to invent something that stopped arguing.

Harvey had to knock three times on Professor Gertie's tower door before she opened it. She was holding a large, yellow duster in each hand. She looked hot and busy.

Harvey told her about his list. But Professor Gertie didn't even look at the notebook Harvey was holding up. "You can't solve everything with a list, Harvey!" she snapped. "I should know that!"

Harvey heard banging from inside the tower. It sounded like an elephant jumping on a trampoline, and Harvey guessed that Mark 1 was bouncing up and down on the couch again. Professor Gertie roared and started back up the stairs into the tower. "Mark 1!" she hollered. "You are *supposed* to be cleaning your room!"

Harvey tore the list from his notebook and stuck it on a nail on Professor Gertie's door. There was nothing else he could do. Then he jogged down Baker Street to his school at the bottom of the hill.

Walking home from school that afternoon, Harvey heard a huge bang. He looked up the hill and saw a swirl of rainbow-colored smoke rising from Professor Gertie's tower.

Harvey ran. When he reached the tower, there was already a crowd of people staring at it. The roof had completely blown off. Harvey looked about frantically.

In a shady spot by the side of the tower, two people were having a picnic.

"What happened?" Harvey asked breath-
lessly as he ran over. "Are you okay? What
happened?"

"You've already asked that," said Professor
Gertie, as Mark 1 poured her a cup of tea. Then
she picked up an oilcan and oiled behind
Mark 1's neck. Mark 1 shivered happily.

"One good turn deserves another," said
Professor Gertie. "And all's well that ends well."

"Huh?" asked Harvey, who was still
wondering what was going on.

"We just had a silly, silly tiff," Professor
Gertie explained. "I decided to clean Mark 1's
room myself. So Mark 1 decided to clean my

Inventing Bench. Some chemicals got mixed together, and there was a small explosion."

"Boom!" said Mark 1 happily, clapping his hands together.

"It made us realize we *had* to stop arguing," said Professor Gertie. "Arguing is DANGEROUS. But we had no idea how to stop — until we found your clever list!"

She held up the page Harvey had torn from his notebook. "You've added two more ideas," said Harvey.

"Not me," said Professor Gertie. "Mark 1 wrote those. Well done, both of you!"

Harvey couldn't believe it. Had his list really made them stop arguing?

"We've decided to do everything as a team," said Professor Gertie. "That way, no one gets left out, and everything is fair." She took a piece of paper from her pocket, and Harvey saw that she and Mark 1 had made a list of their own. "Mark 1's going to have his own Inventing Bench next to mine," she said. "We'll each do half of the housework and laundry. And from now on we'll *both* coach The Team."

"If there is a Team," Harvey said miserably.

"But you know how to fix The Team's problems now, don't you?" asked Professor Gertie. "Use your list!"

Harvey took the list from Professor Gertie, folded it up and put it in his pocket.

"It won't work," he said.

"Trry itt!" said Mark 1 as he buttered a scone and handed it to Professor Gertie.

Harvey still couldn't believe they were getting along so well. Maybe — just maybe — the list would work for The Team.

"Okay, I'll try it," he said, and for the first time all week, he managed a hopeful smile.

Chapter 5

On Saturday morning, Harvey woke up to the sound of rain hammering on his bedroom window. He groaned. Just the sort of weather to put everyone in a bad mood.

He splashed through puddles to the field, his soggy socks squishing, and all his hope evaporating. There was no way The Team would follow his stupid list. If he read it to them, everyone would laugh, and then he might as well walk straight home again.

When he arrived at the field, he saw Rita warming up. "You're back!" he said. "What happened?"

"I didn't want to give in to Steffi and Matt," Rita said. "I'm a match for their insults any day — I'll just argue back!"

Harvey didn't like the sound of that. "Maybe you won't have to argue," he said.

While he waited for the rest of The Team to arrive, Harvey watched the Diamonds warming up. They looked organized and happy, like they knew they were going to win.

Harvey called The Team into a huddle. "I've got a plan," he said.

"Here we go," said Matt, pretending to yawn.

"This game is really important," Harvey continued. "If we want to win the league, *and* a trip to Soccer Camp, we either have to tie or win this game."

"We already know that!" said Steffi scornfully.

"But if we keep arguing," Harvey went on, "we won't win anything. There won't even *be* a team anymore. We've got to stop arguing!"

"Good plan," sniggered Matt. "I think that's *really* going to work, don't you, Steffi?"

Ignoring Matt, Harvey took a deep breath and read them his list.

How to Stop Arguing and Be a Team
1. Ask, don't tell.
2. Discuss our problems.
3. Be positive and don't criticize.

Then he read them what Mark 1 had added:

4. No nagging!
5. Bee happee!

Matt took the list from him. "So this is your great plan?"

"Yes," said Harvey.

Matt started to laugh. "Harvey, you're so funny!"

"Come on," said Steffi impatiently. "The ref's waiting. We don't have time for Harvey's jokes."

The Team took their positions, with Matt still laughing loudly.

"Too bad, Harvey," said Rita as she headed for her goal. "Good try."

Harvey shrugged. He saw Professor Gertie and Mark 1 arrive together, chatting happily under a shared umbrella. At least the list had worked for them. But he still felt miserable. He was sure he was about to play his last-ever game with The Team.

Chapter 6

The Diamonds kicked off, and Harvey chased after the ball, skidding and slipping in the mud. Finally, Steffi got the ball with a sliding tackle. She darted forward and was knocked over by a Diamonds defender. The ref awarded her a free kick in line with the Diamonds' goal.

"You take it," Steffi ordered Matt. "You're a better shot than me."

Matt looked furious. "How dare you tell me what to do!" he shouted. But as he turned away, Harvey saw him grin secretly.

Matt turned back to Steffi and declared, "Ask, don't tell!"

"Okay, okay!" said Steffi crossly. "Matt, would you please take this free kick?"

"Let's discuss it," said Matt, folding his arms. "That's what the list says to do, Steffi. I'm trying to help you here."

The Diamonds were laughing.

Steffi's face turned red. "Just take the free kick!" she yelled. "Why do you have to be so difficult all the time?"

Matt grinned and quoted from the list again. "Be positive and don't criticize."

Rita, who'd run up the field to see what the argument was about, tried to hide a smile behind her gloves. "And no nagging!" she reminded Steffi.

"Don't forget to bee happee!" finished Matt, who was laughing so hard he couldn't stand.

The rest of The Team were laughing too — all except Steffi, who was fuming, and Harvey, who was frowning thoughtfully. The Team were laughing instead of arguing. Had his list done that?

"That's enough!" said the ref. "The free kick can go to the Diamonds instead!"

The Diamonds took the kick quickly, and The Team ran back to defend. Rita reached her

goal just in time. A Diamonds attacker was
bearing down on her, drawing back his foot to
shoot.

Steffi skidded into him, stopping the shot,
but the ref's whistle screamed — the
Diamonds had another free kick, this time
right in front of Rita's goal.

While Harvey arranged a wall, Rita
crouched low, keeping her eyes on the ball.

"That's good," said Darren. "But stand up
more and think big. It looks like he's going to
blast it."

Rita turned her head. Darren was beside the goal. "You're back!" she said.

"Only to watch," said Darren.

"But your purple splotches have gone," said Rita. "You could play."

"Have The Team stopped arguing?" asked Darren.

"We haven't argued for at least a minute," said Rita.

"Well, that's a world record," said Darren grimly. Then he pointed, "Quick!"

Rita turned too late. The Diamonds defender had already blasted the ball straight at her, and it hit her square in the forehead.

Rita stumbled backwards and sat down in the mud.

The ball flew up into the air and came straight down again. This time it hit her on the top of the head and bounced backwards into the goal.

The Diamonds cheered.

"Rita!" yelled Steffi, standing over her as the rest of The Team ran up. Steffi's face had twisted in what Harvey thought was rage. But instead of shouting, Steffi started making a noise like a chicken clucking. At first, no one knew what she was doing.

"Is she laughing?" asked Harvey at last.

"It's hard to tell," said Matt. "But I think so."

"I was wrong when I said Darren was useless!" Steffi spluttered. "Next to Rita, he's a genius!" She tried to pull Rita to her feet, still clucking madly.

"I'm glad you see the funny side," said Rita, smiling. "I know I'm hopeless, and I wish we had a good goalie, but we don't."

"Yes we do," Steffi said, turning to Darren. "I'm sorry for what I said," she told him seriously. "But now we've got this crazy list that stops us from arguing. It makes us laugh instead! So will you come back now, Darren? Please?"

Harvey was sure Darren would shake his head and walk away. He kept remembering Darren's face covered in purple splotches. But to Harvey's surprise, Darren took off his jacket. He was wearing his goalkeeper's shirt underneath.

"I'll need my gloves," he told Rita. "You get back on attack, where you belong."

The Team all cheered as Darren took his place in goal, and Harvey began to get excited. The Team were back! And if they played their best, they'd be good enough to win …

Harvey kicked off, and The Team kept the ball, passing it around.

Slowly, they edged towards the Diamonds' goal.

Soon Rita was in position to shoot. She drew back her foot, then smiled and passed to Matt instead. "Would you like to take this shot, my good sir?" she asked politely.

"Why thank you, madam." Matt took a swipe at the ball, and it skidded towards the corner flag.

"Useless," said Rita, shaking her head. "Oh no — sorry, I meant to say excellent try, Matt!"

Steffi laughed. So did Matt. But Harvey was annoyed. They'd had a chance, and they'd wasted it.

Harvey managed to intercept the ball and start another attack. He passed to Matt.

"Ladies first," said Matt. He passed it straight to Steffi.

"Thanks," said Steffi lightly. "But I think Harvey should have it. He *is* our captain, after all."

"What are you doing?" complained Harvey. Diamonds players were swarming around him. He managed to flick the ball over their heads to Rita, who had a clear path ahead.

But Rita passed it straight back to him, even though he was still surrounded.

"Why don't you do one of your brilliant runs?" Rita encouraged him. "You know, where you take on the whole defense and score."

Harvey twisted and turned his way through the Diamonds. To his surprise, he still had the ball at his feet. He looked around for someone to pass to, but they were all too busy laughing. Harvey couldn't believe it. He was glad that they weren't arguing anymore, but now they were joking around so much they weren't taking the game seriously!

Harvey put on some speed to outrun a Diamonds midfielder. He was heading towards the Diamonds' goal. But there were so many Diamonds players in his way that there was no where to go except straight at them.

Harvey slowed down, turning left, right, pushing the ball through defenders' legs until he stumbled and started to fall. He felt a sudden anger at The Team. Why couldn't they just play like they used to? If they'd helped him, instead of standing around laughing, they might have had a goal.

As Harvey tumbled to the ground, he stretched and wildly kicked the ball away. The Diamonds goalie cried out in dismay as the ball shot into his goal.

The Team went wild, skidding through the mud towards Harvey.

"When we enjoy ourselves, we're the best!" declared Steffi.

"But we have to play *correctly*," Harvey urged them. "If we do that, we can have fun *and* win!"

The Diamonds kicked off, attacking fiercely, and The Team settled down in defense. At half-time the score was still 1-1.

Harvey was glowing. "If the score stays like this, we'll win the league!" he said. "And ..."

"No," said Steffi. "If we win, we win. But if we start thinking about it, we'll only get nervous and start arguing again."

"Forget about winning," said Matt.

But Harvey couldn't forget about it.

The second half started like the first had ended, with the Diamonds attacking furiously. The Team were worn out from defending and had hardly any energy left to attack. But they held on, and at last Harvey saw the ref check his watch.

Harvey almost cheered. The Team were going to tie the game and win the league!

Matt cleared the ball from defense, and Harvey collected it. He turned to attack, dodged a defender, then shouted in frustration when the defender tackled him.

"Cool it," Rita said as she ran back to defend again. "Remember, be happy!"

Harvey was too nervous to be happy. The Team only had to keep the Diamonds from scoring for another few minutes!

The Diamonds defender kicked the ball high and long over everyone's heads. Darren held up his arms to catch it after it bounced.

But the ball didn't bounce.

It landed with a slap in the swampy goal area, skidded through Darren's legs, and trickled into the goal.

It was the worst goalkeeping mistake Harvey had ever seen. Without thinking, he raced towards Darren. He wasn't going to wait for The Team to start shouting — this time, he was going to do it himself!

Chapter 7

Harvey tore down the field. Darren had lost them everything. They'd have been better off without him.

But as he reached the goal area, Harvey started to slip. He fell onto his back with a SPLAT! and shot across the watery mud, which sloshed up the legs of his shorts and inside his shirt but didn't slow him down. Just like the ball had a minute before, Harvey skidded straight through Darren's legs.

When he stood up, he had to spit out a mouthful of mud. He used his little fingers to clear mud from his ears — and then he heard The Team roaring with laughter.

"I'm not complaining," said Steffi, who was standing over Darren shaking her head. "But that was TERRIBLE!" She started clucking so hard she was barely able to breathe.

"It wasn't a very good save, was it?" said Darren, shaking his head. "I couldn't even save Harvey!"

Harvey started to giggle. He felt mud trickling down his ribs and squeezing its way out in lumps from his shorts, and he laughed. He had to keep stopping to spit out more mud, but thinking about how he'd skidded through Darren's legs made him start laughing all over again. It felt like all his anger was rising harmlessly into the sky like the rainbow-colored smoke from Professor Gertie's tower, leaving him warm and happy.

"It's not your fault," he said to Darren. "It must be like goalkeeping on an ice rink."

"It's worse," said Darren. "But I'm sorry we're going to lose."

"Don't worry," said Harvey. "The Team are cured, and that's all that matters."

The ref blew his whistle and checked his watch again, as The Team kicked off. The Diamonds stayed back in defense.

"One minute to go!" yelled Professor Gertie and Mark 1 together through the Shouting Mask.

Harvey watched them jumping up and down, and was twice as glad that they were enjoying themselves so much. The Team didn't have to win. All they had to do was play together and be happy.

Rita had the ball. There were a lot of Diamonds players between her and the Diamonds' goal.

"Your turn to score," said Harvey with a friendly smile.

Rita laughed. Her legs always turned to jelly when she got near the goal. Everyone knew that. But now that there was no pressure, she might as well have some fun.

She approached the defenders slowly, as if she was trying to work out a way through the maze of legs.

"Yes!" Harvey shouted as Rita passed one defender, then he clapped as she skipped past two more.

CRUNCH! Harvey winced, but Rita was still on her feet, and she was inside the Diamonds' goal area. Suddenly, Harvey felt a jolt of excitement. There was a space opening up in front of the goal. If Rita bore left, she'd have a clear shot!

Harvey tried not to think about it. If she scored, she scored. He watched her burst through two defenders into the space he had seen. She only had the goalie to beat. She lined up the shot and…

"Ow!" Rita yelled in pain as a defender crashed into her from behind, sending her crashing into the mud.

Harvey had no idea why The Team were cheering as he helped Rita to her feet. Then he heard the ref blow his whistle, and turned to see him pointing to the penalty spot.

Harvey felt a hundred butterflies flutter inside his stomach. They had a penalty!

"Harvey takes it!" said Rita, grinning as she limped back towards the rest of The Team.

Harvey's stomach lurched. His face felt hot and cold, and he kept touching it to see if he could feel any purple splotches. "It's not my penalty!" he pleaded.

"You take it, Rita," said Steffi. "It's yours."

Rita went pale. "No. I can't. You take it."

Steffi folded her arms tightly. "Uh-uh. Matt can take it."

"No way!" said Matt.

The ref looked at his watch.

"Someone take the penalty!" Harvey said desperately. "The ref might take it away!"

Everyone was frowning and looking angry. Was this the end of The Team after all, arguing over who would take the most important penalty they'd ever had? Harvey couldn't believe it, but he knew he didn't have the nerve to take it — and neither did anyone else.

Darren trotted over. "What's the problem?" he asked. "If no one else wants to take it, I will."

The Team all gasped. "What about the pressure?" asked Harvey.

"Taking this penalty is *good* pressure," said Darren. "If I score, we win and I'm a hero. If I miss, no one can complain because no one else wants to take it. Right?"

The Team all nodded.

Darren placed the ball on the penalty spot. He waited for the ref to blow his whistle, then he took two steps up to the ball and blasted it.

"**Goal!**" screamed Professor Gertie and Mark 1.

But the Diamonds goalkeeper pushed the ball to the side, where it hit the goalpost and rebounded back out — straight to Darren.

This time, Darren calmly fired the ball straight into the center of the goal.

The Team were stunned to silence.

"No problem," said Darren as the final whistle was blown. "Soccer Camp, here we come!"

Professor
Gertie

Darren

Harvey

Rita

Matt

Steffi

Mark 1